What's Mine Is Mine

What's Mine Is Mine

A Book About Sharing

By Barbara Shook Hazen
Illustrated by Barbara Steadman

*Prepared with the cooperation of Bernice Berk, Ph.D.,
of the Bank Street College of Education*

A GOLDEN BOOK · NEW YORK
Western Publishing Company, Inc., Racine, Wisconsin 53404

Note to Parents

The sharing of our possessions, ideas, and feelings plays an important part in coexisting with others, whether it be within a family setting, a classroom, or a group of co-workers.

When children are young, their parents often encourage them to share toys, food, and other things. Yet the concept of sharing does not exist when children are commanded or pressured, rather than encouraged, to share.

Children do need to experience ownership of some things in order to learn to respect their property and that of others. Even in family situations, where a room, toys, books, and even clothes may be shared with siblings, there still should be something special that belongs to each child alone. But it's also important that children develop an appreciation of the pleasures and rewards of sharing, that is, that others will share with them. Once they do, they are more likely to become adults who are truly giving.

—The Editors

At school, Laura was good at sharing. She didn't take more than her fair time at the computer.

She liked sharing her lunch cookies with her friends...

...except when her mother baked butterscotch fudgies. Those were her absolute favorite. Then, the most she felt like sharing was "one bite."

Laura was pretty good at sharing at school parties. She took her turn whacking the piñata.

And she didn't scalp all the cheese topping off the chicken casserole in the food line.

Laura was good at sharing with children all over the world who didn't have as much as she had.

It made her feel good to put coins in the World Hunger box, and wrap and recycle her toys for others.

Laura never had trouble sharing with her cousin, Jim. They liked each other, but not each other's things.

Jim liked snakes, which Laura couldn't stand. And Laura liked making robots, which Jim didn't understand.

The one thing they shared was a love of books. So they traded the ones they'd finished with each other, which was nice.

Laura had a little brother, Bill. Sometimes she felt like sharing with him. It made her feel giving and good inside when he smiled and said, "Mmmm, thanks, Laura."

Of course, she didn't always feel like sharing with Bill.
Sometimes he didn't share fairly—like the time he took out
all the purple jelly beans, which were *her* favorite, too.
Other times, she just didn't feel like sharing at all.

Laura especially didn't feel like sharing the things that were personal, or precious, or important to her. She didn't feel like sharing the writing paper with her name on it, or her special books. She didn't like to share her colored pencils because Bill always mushed the points and Laura liked her points to be sharp.

Laura didn't feel like sharing most of the things in her room because her room was her private place. She felt mad and invaded when Bill sneaked in and messed up her desk— which she liked just so—or fooled around with her things without asking.

It made her so mad, she felt like knocking all the toys off his shelves to get even.

Instead, she said, "What's mine is mine, and you stay away unless I say it's okay!"

"What's mine is mine!" Laura told Bill the day he wanted to play with her Space Robot. "Play with something else!"

It was a special birthday gift from her grandmother, because Laura liked robots and wanted to be a robot maker someday. It was also easily broken, and Bill didn't know how to make it work.

Laura was afraid her mother would make her share her
Space Robot. But she didn't.

"Laura's right," she told Bill. "What's hers *is* hers. Just as
what's yours is yours. You don't have to share the things that
belong to you—unless you feel like it. They're not like TV, or
playing cards, or cherry pies, which are supposed to be shared.

"Sometimes it's nice to share your things." Their mother
put an arm around them both. "But that's up to you to decide."

"Well, I don't want to share my Space Robot," said Laura. "It's new, and Bill always breaks my things. But mainly because it's mine!"

"It's up to you," Laura's mother said again. "Bill can help me bake a pie while you play."

Then she said, "But I suggest you play in your room, and put your robot away when you're finished playing."

Laura did. But the next day, when their mother had a
meeting and she and Bill had a new sitter, Laura forgot.

She marched her Space Robot right in front of Bill, who was
watching monster cartoons on TV.

"I want a turn. I want to play. Please let me play,"
Bill begged.

"No, it's mine," Laura said.

"Laura, it's not nice not to share," the new baby-sitter said.
"Now, share nicely."

Laura was annoyed. She shared. But it was because someone was making her do it, not because she felt like it. She wished her mother were there to help her stick up for her rights!

Bill made a smug face and turned the control knob to the left.

"That's the wrong way!" Laura yelled.

She shoved Bill as she leapt after her Space Robot, which was heading right for the living room wall.

There was a big crash. The robot's arm fell off, and Laura burst into furious tears.

"Now see what you've done! You've ruined everything," Laura lashed out at her brother.

She switched off Bill's TV show and stomped to her room. "See if I ever share anything with you again," she said.

"That isn't a nice thing to say," said the baby-sitter.

"I don't feel nice!" said Laura, who felt mad and miserable.

She felt a little better when her mother got home. Laura's mother hugged her and said the baby-sitter didn't use good judgment in what she said, and in *making* Laura share. She also said the Space Robot could be fixed as good as new—and fixed it before she did anything else.

She realized how important this very special gift was to Laura.

Now Bill was the one who felt miserable. He stood in the doorway with tear streaks on his face, and a fistful of purple jelly beans from the bag he bought with the pennies from his piggy bank.

"I'm sorry," he said to Laura. Then he said, "Here, you can have them all."

"I've got a better idea," said Laura, hugging her little
brother. "Why don't we share them."

That was just what they did.

And a little later, after Laura showed Bill how to work the Space Robot, she shared that, too. She let Bill play with it for a few minutes.

Laura felt better about sharing her things *when* it was her idea.

The more Laura shared, the more Bill started sharing back.
He also started to stay away from Laura's things, except when
she said, "Want to play with my paints?" or "Want a piece?"

Laura shared more and more—and not because someone
made her do it. She shared because *she* wanted to, and
because she knew she didn't *always* have to share, and
because it *was* up to her.